Girls Play to Win

SWIMMING & DIVING

by Paul Hoblin

Content Consultant
John Naber
Olympic Swimming Champion
and Broadcaster

NorwoodHouse Press
CHICAGO, ILLINOIS

Norwood House Press
P.O. Box 316598
Chicago, Illinois 60631

For information regarding Norwood House Press, please visit our website at
www.norwoodhousepress.com or call 866-565-2900.

Photo Credits: Herbert Kratky/Shutterstock Images, cover; Itsuo Inouye/AP Images, 4; Alex Bramwell/Bigstock, 6; Susan Leggett/Bigstock, 8; Bigstock, 11; iStockphoto, 13, 26; George Grantham Bain Collection/Library of Congress, 14, 15; Popperfoto/Getty Images, 17; AP Images, 18, 21, 36, 39; Goran Milic/Bigstock, 23; Mark Duncan/AP Images, 25; Brian McEntire/iStockphoto, 28; Shutterstock Images, 31; Nicolaas Traut/Bigstock, 32; Marcello Farina/Shutterstock Images, 35; Amy Sancetta/AP Images, 40; Santiago Lyon/AP Images, 42; Tom Strattman/AP Images, 45; Petros Giannakouris/AP Images, 47; Luis M. Alvarez/AP Images, 48; David Longstreath/AP Images, 50; Mark J. Terrill/AP Images, 51; Xiao Yong/Imaginechina/AP Images, 53; Anja Niedringhaus/AP Images, 57; Paul Hoblin, 64 (top); John Naber, 64 (bottom)

Editor: Chrös McDougall
Series Design and cover production: Christa Schneider
Interior production: Craig Hinton

Library of Congress Cataloging-in-Publication Data

Hoblin, Paul.
Girls play to win swimming & diving / by Paul Hoblin.
p. cm. -- (Girls play to win)
Includes bibliographical references and index.
Summary: "Covers the history, rules, fundamentals, and significant personalities of the sport of women's swimming and diving. Topics include: techniques, strategies, competitive events, and equipment. Glossary, Additional Resources, and Index included"--Provided by publisher.
ISBN-13: 978-1-59953-466-4 (library edition : alk. paper)
ISBN-10: 1-59953-466-5 (library edition : alk. paper)
1. Swimming for women--Juvenile literature. 2. Diving for women--Juvenile literature. 3. Swimming for children--Juvenile literature. I. Title.
GV837.5.H63 2011
797.2'1082--dc22

2011011038

Manufactured in the United States of America in North Mankato, Minnesota.
177N—072011

Girls Play to Win

SWIMMING & DIVING

Table of Contents

CHAPTER 1 Swimming Basics 4

CHAPTER 2 Getting Started 14

CHAPTER 3 Swimming to Victory 18

CHAPTER 4 Diving Basics 26

CHAPTER 5 Diving In 36

CHAPTER 6 Perfect Entry 42

CHAPTER 7 Playing to Win 48

Glossary 58
For More Information 60
Index 62
Places to Visit 64
About the Author and Content Consultant 64

Words in **bold type** are defined in the glossary.

▲ *Dara Torres leaves the starting block in the 50-meter freestyle at the 2008 Olympic Games.*

CHAPTER 1 SWIMMING BASICS

Like the other women standing on the starting blocks, Dara Torres bent at the waist as she waited for the horn to sound. She had the same muscular arms and legs as her competitors. Under her swim cap and behind her goggles, she looked basically the same as every other swimmer. But she wasn't the same.

For one thing, she was older. A lot older. At 41, Torres had been swimming for almost two decades before some of her competitors were even born. She first competed in the Olympic Games in 1984. Now, at the 2008 Games in Beijing, China, she was competing in the Olympic Games for her fifth time.

Torres's age wasn't the only reason she stood out from the other swimmers. She was also faster than almost all of them. She had already won two silver medals in the 2008 Games. That had made her the oldest swimmer to ever win even one medal. Now she wanted to win a third medal, this time in the 50-meter freestyle.

When the horn sounded, Torres dove into the water. It took just 24.07 seconds for her to touch the opposite wall. That was fast enough for second place, giving Torres her third silver medal of those Games and her 12th Olympic medal overall. With that, Torres tied a record for the most medals won by a U.S. woman swimmer. And she wasn't ready to stop there.

GETTING STARTED

Torres specializes in "freestyle" events. Technically, a competitor is allowed to perform any of the four swimming strokes during a freestyle event. However, since the **front crawl** is the fastest stroke, it is the stroke of choice in these events. In fact, many people simply refer to the front crawl as the freestyle. To do the freestyle, a

▲ *This swimmer does the front crawl, also known as the freestyle. It is the fastest swimming stroke.*

swimmer scissor-kicks with her legs. She alternates her arms like a windmill. To breathe, she turns her head to the opposite side of the arm that's entering the water.

The other three swimming strokes are the **backstroke**, the **breaststroke**, and the **butterfly**. The backstroke is similar to the freestyle, only the swimmer lies on her back in the water. Like the freestyle, she scissor-kicks with her feet and alternates backward windmill-like arm pulls.

To do the breaststroke, the swimmer mimics a frog's kick with her legs and feet. She pulls the water back with

Freestyle

As the fastest stroke, the freestyle is now the clear choice for all freestyle events. But this wasn't always the case. For hundreds of years the stroke of choice in Europe was the breaststroke. Several books were written during that time about swimming, and all of them assumed that the breaststroke was the truest form of the sport. It wasn't until 1844, at a competition in London, England, that Europeans were first introduced to the freestyle. Two Native Americans, Flying Gull and Tobacco, used the freestyle to tear through the water and easily beat their European competitors.

her arms while kicking the water out with her legs. To go as fast as possible, her feet and legs must always be moving in symmetry, or at the same time.

In the butterfly, the swimmer uses her legs to copy a dolphin's movement. Her feet and legs must be pressed together and moving at the same time. Her arms **recover** over the water, both at the same time.

Usually, these four strokes are used in separate races. The only time they're combined is during a **medley**. That is when one swimmer or a team of swimmers must swim every stroke once. For example, a swimmer might switch strokes each time she touches the wall.

▲ *Swimmers cheer on their teammates during a relay race. Once the active swimmer touches the wall, the next swimmer on her team begins.*

SWIM RACES

Depending on the pool, the distance of each event can be measured in yards or meters. However, most official races—including the Olympic Games—use meters. An Olympic-size pool is 50 meters long, although 25-meter and 25-yard pools are also common. Swimming from one end of the pool to the other is called a **length**. Swimming from one end of the pool to the other and then back (two lengths) is called a **lap**.

Open Water Swimming

Open water swimming races take place in natural bodies of water, such as lakes or oceans. Races are often much longer than traditional pool races, sometimes reaching as many as 25,000 meters, or approximately 15.5 miles. However, open water swimming can be dangerous and should not be attempted without proper training and supervision.

When a freestyle swimmer reaches the end of the pool and needs to reverse her direction, she can do a **flip turn**. As the swimmer approaches the wall, she does a somersault in the water and pushes off the wall with her feet. Flip turns are only allowed when swimming the free-style or the backstroke. During breaststroke and butterfly races, a swimmer must touch the wall with her hands, or she will be disqualified.

SWIMMING EQUIPMENT

All you really need to swim is a swimsuit and water. However, almost every competitive swimmer also uses goggles and a swim cap. Swim caps cover the hair and reduce **drag.** That helps the swimmer move faster through the water.

Swimmers often use other equipment to help train and take care of their bodies. There are buoys, kickboards,

The Events

The events in a swim meet depend on the competition and the size of the pool. At the Olympic Games, women swimmers compete in individual races at 50, 100, 200, 400, and 800 meters, depending on the stroke. There are also 200- and 400-meter **individual medleys (IMs)** as well as three team relays: 4x100 meter freestyle, 4x200 meter freestyle, and 4x100 meter medley. The 2008 Olympic Games also added a 10,000-meter open water race.

fins, and paddles that help a swimmer practice a specific stroke. There are also skin and hair care products that can be applied before or after practice. However, come race time, all a swimmer really needs is a suit, goggles, and a swim cap.

Swimsuits have changed throughout the years in an effort to increase speed. Some companies have designed special bodysuits that allow competitors to swim faster and faster. As these high-tech suits continued to improve during the early 2000s, world records began to fall regularly. It also gave swimmers with better swimsuits an advantage. So after the 2009 season, the international body that governs swimming banned full-body swimsuits from competition.

▲ *A swim cap helps this swimmer move faster through the water while she does the breaststroke.*

So Much Speed

The 2009 World Championships showed off the advantages of the high-tech polyurethane swimsuits. In the men's 100-meter freestyle quarterfinals, 16 swimmers finished as fast as the winner of the event in 2007.

A GREAT, HEALTHY SPORT

Swimming is a sport that can be enjoyed on a recreational or competitive level at just about any age. As Torres said, "The water doesn't know what age you are." Whether you're 60, 16, or six, performing each swim stroke requires skill and coordination. It's also a great way to get exercise. Plus, once you get in a rhythm in the pool, swimming can offer you time to think through problems at home or at school, or to clear your mind completely and relax. Many people find the ability to feel weightless on the water to be very relaxing.

Most importantly, swimming is fun. More than 52 million people do it at least six times per year, and that's just in the United States.

▲ *This swimmer gets ready to dive into the water for a swim.*

▲ *Swimmers prepare for the women's 100-yard swim at the Coney Island Races around 1910.*

CHAPTER 2

GETTING STARTED

People have been swimming for thousands of years. Artwork in an Egyptian tomb depicts someone doing what looks like the freestyle. The Assyrians, another ancient civilization, carved a statue of a swimmer doing the breaststroke. In fact, similar drawings of swimmers exist from several of the earliest cultures.

The first known competitive swimming races took place in Japan in 36 BC. That means people have been racing each other through the water for more than 2,000 years.

MODERN OLYMPIC GAMES

The ancient Olympic Games in Greece did not include swimming races. The modern Olympic Games began in 1896. Swimming was one of the original sports in the modern Olympic Games. Yet even then, the races did not look much like the ones we know today.

The very first Olympic swim race consisted of three Greek sailors jumping out of a rowboat and swimming across a bay. The next Olympic Games took place in 1900. There, competitors swam up

Three young women pose in their swimsuits during the early 20th century.

WHAT TO WEAR?

Australian Fanny Durack might have proven that women belonged in the pool by winning a gold medal at the 1912 Olympic Games, but what women could and could not wear once they were in the pool remained a source of controversy. Ethelda Bleibtrey was the first woman to beat Durack in a swim race. But in 1919, Bleibtrey was arrested for "nude swimming." Her crime sounds more shocking than it was: All she had done was remove her stockings before diving into the water!

Professional Competitions

Fanny Durack was the first superstar of women's swimming. She won her first swim race in 1906, when she was 17 years old. Many people shunned women's swimming during that time, but that only motivated the rebellious swimmer. Besides winning the first Olympic gold medal in women's swimming, the Australian also set world records in the 100-yard freestyle, the 100-meter freestyle, the 220-yard freestyle, the 500-meter freestyle, and the mile. Durack also traveled the world to promote women's swimming. After being inducted into the International Swimming Hall of Fame, the Hall noted in her bio that "no one did more to dominate women's swimming longer than Australian Fanny Durack."

a river and around obstacles that had intentionally been placed in their way. In another race, they were expected to swim the entire distance underwater.

Women were allowed to compete in some sports during the early years of the Olympic Games. However, they were not allowed to take part in these early Olympic swimming races. At the time, many people believed that women were too frail to swim in competitive events. They saw swimming as too vigorous for women. They also thought it was an unladylike activity.

It was not until 1912 that the women were finally allowed to swim at the Olympic Games. The only women's event that year was the 100-meter freestyle. Australian

▲ *Gold medalist Fanny Durack (left) stands with Australian silver medalist Mina Wylie (center) and British bronze medalist Jennie Fletcher following the 100-meter freestyle at the 1912 Olympic Games.*

Fanny Durack won the gold medal. However, she almost did not get that opportunity.

At first, the New South Wales Ladies' Amateur Swimming Association had tried to ban Durack from competing at the Olympic Games. According to the association, women were not allowed to appear in competitions when men were present. The public disagreed, though. People demanded that Durack get a chance to show off her talent in the water. And that is exactly what she did.

Between 1912 and 1918, Durack broke 11 world records. Later, she was inducted into the International Swimming Hall of Fame in Fort Lauderdale, Florida. Durack was the first great female swimming champion. Many, many other women have been swimming for gold ever since.

▲ *Dawn Fraser (center) stands atop the podium after winning the women's 100-meter freestyle event at the 1960 Olympic Games.*

CHAPTER 3 SWIMMING TO VICTORY

Many great women have swum in the Olympic Games since 1912. Perhaps the greatest was Australian Dawn Fraser. She was the fastest female swimmer in the world for more than a decade. Fraser won gold medals in the 100-meter freestyle at three straight Olympic Games: 1956, 1960, and 1964.

Many people considered Fraser to have been past her prime when she arrived at the 1964 Olympic Games at age 27. She proved them wrong when she not only won the 100-meter freestyle but also set a world record that stood until 1972. Although it might not sound like a long time, eight years is practically an eternity for a swimming record.

Fraser was so dominant in the pool that she made winning look easy. It wasn't. In fact, she only really began swimming because she had asthma, a disease that makes it hard to breathe. "I was an asthmatic," she said, "and knew swimming was good for my health."

Fraser also dealt with issues outside of swimming. The 1964 Games were in Tokyo, Japan. Eight months before those Games, Fraser and her mother were in a car accident that left her mother dead and Fraser badly injured. Fraser was devastated. She had to wear a neck brace for months after the crash. But her determination in the pool never wavered. Fraser managed to win another gold medal and set the world record later that year.

Fraser ended her career with four Olympic gold medals and four Olympic silver medals. In 1999, the World Sport Awards named her World Athlete of the Century and the Australian Sports Hall of Fame named her Athlete of the Century.

More Trouble

Dawn Fraser survived the car accident before the 1964 Olympic Games, but more trouble brewed once she got to the Games in Tokyo, Japan. Once there, she was arrested for trying to steal an Olympic flag outside Emperor Hirohito's palace. She was not charged, and Japanese officials gave her the flag as a souvenir. But the Australian Swimming Union (ASU) was already upset with Fraser for marching in the Opening Ceremony despite a team-wide ban on doing so. The flag incident pushed the ASU over the edge. It suspended Fraser from swimming for 10 years. Eventually, public outcry overturned the suspension—but it was too late. With only a few months remaining until the 1968 Olympic Games, Fraser didn't have time to train for another gold.

TRACY CAULKINS

The future looked bright for U.S. swimmer Tracy Caulkins. She was only 15 years old when she arrived at the 1978 World Championships in Berlin, West Germany. Yet Caulkins won five gold medals and one silver medal. Her best events were the 200- and 400-meter individual medleys (IMs). She was already one of the most versatile athletes in the world.

Caulkins was expected to star at the 1980 Olympic Games in Moscow, Soviet Union (now Russia). However, the United States decided to boycott the Games for political reasons. That meant Tracy had to stay home while

▲ *Tracy Caulkins practices at the Olympic swimming venue before the 1984 Olympic Games in Los Angeles, California.*

other swimmers from other countries competed for medals she otherwise might have won.

All she could do was wait. The next Olympic Games would be in 1984. Caulkins knew that by then she might no longer be at the top of her sport. "I suppose I could be over the hill in 1984," she said at the time.

Her statement might sound too dramatic. After all, Caulkins would be only 21 years old in 1984. But in competitive women's swimming, many of the top athletes are only in their teens.

Over the next few years, Caulkins grew both taller and heavier. Her added size seemed to be slowing her down in the pool. The world records she had set in the 200-meter and 400-meter IMs had been broken. The 1984 Games in

Los Angeles, California, would be Caulkins's last shot to win gold in the Olympic Games.

That is exactly what she did, though. In fact, she won three times. By the end of the 1984 Games, Caulkins had gold medals in the 400-meter IM, the 200-meter IM, and the 4x100 medley relay. All that waiting had finally paid off for Tracy Caulkins.

KRISTIN OTTO

The United States and Australia have generally been the superpowers in women's swimming since the sport's beginning. From 1976 to 1988, however, the East Germans dominated the sport. At the 1988 Olympic Games, for example, East Germany won 10 of the 15 gold medals given to female swimmers.

The Olympic Games are supposed to be free of politics. However, that has not always been the case. Prior to the U.S.-led boycott of the 1980 Olympic Games in the Soviet Union, countries had refused to participate in the Games of 1956 and 1976. In 1984, when Tracy Caulkins won her three gold medals, she did so without having to compete against her biggest rivals, the East Germans, because their country was boycotting the Games.

The country's greatest champion was Kristin Otto. She swam in six events at the 1988 Games. She won gold medals in every one. Her six gold medals in one Olympic Games were an all-time record. In fact, she became the first female athlete to win six gold medals at a single Olympic Games. Just as incredible, Otto beat all her competitors in all four strokes.

"She's best because she works harder than the rest," East German coach Wolfgang Richter said. ". . . She cannot stand to lose."

Otto was no doubt a hard worker. However, coaches and team officials later revealed that she had help in achieving those feats in the form of performance-enhancing drugs (PEDs). PEDs, such as steroids, are illegal drugs that give athletes increased

Illegal PEDs can cause harm to your body and result in bans from competition.

DOPING

Steroid use, and other forms of ***doping****, have been a controversial part of many sports. Although some athletes take these drugs purposely, others do not realize that they are taking illegal drugs. It is important to consult with your doctor before taking any nutritional supplement, both for your health and your eligibility. Fédération Internationale de Natation (FINA), the international governing body of swimming and other water sports, has a section on its website (www.fina.org) devoted to reports and rulings regarding doping cases.*

strength and faster recovery. In a sport decided by fractions of a second, PEDs can make a big difference in the end result.

Otto was not the only one. After East Germany and West Germany united in 1990, many East German athletes confessed that they had been forced to take illegal PEDs for years. Several of these athletes were swimmers.

Steroids and other PEDs can make athletes faster in the pool. But they also have many negative side effects. They can cause liver cancer and other types of organ damage. These drugs can also cause psychological problems and the inability to have children.

The achievements of many East German swimmers in the 1970s and 1980s were tarnished. However, there have been many great German swimmers who have never been linked to performance-enhancing drugs. Among them were Franziska van Almsick and Hannah Stockbauer. They were each winners of *Swimming World Magazine*'s Swimmer of the Year Award. But as a country, Germany is no longer the great power of women's swimming that it once was.

JANET EVANS

At 5 feet 5 inches (1.7 m) tall and weighing around 100 pounds (45.4 kg), U.S. swimmer Janet Evans often looked like her competitors' kid sister. In some cases, she was

▲ *Janet Evans backstrokes during a preliminary race in the women's 400-meter IM at the Seoul Olympic Games in 1988.*

young enough to be just that. Evans was 15 years old in 1987 when she broke the world records in the 400-, the 800-, and the 1,500-meter freestyle.

A little more than a year later, Evans became one of Team USA's stars at the 1988 Olympic Games. In Seoul, South Korea, she won gold medals in the 400-meter IM, the 400-meter freestyle, and the 800-meter freestyle. She also went home with a nickname: Miss Perpetual Motion. The name fit her rapid movement in the water and her relentless, unusual straight-armed recovery.

Evans collected more medals at the 1992 Olympic Games in Barcelona, Spain. She won a gold medal in the 800-meter freestyle and a silver medal in the 400-meter freestyle. When she retired, she held three world records. Many consider her to be the greatest distance swimmer in U.S. history.

▲ *This springboard diver jumps in preparation for a dive.*

CHAPTER 4

DIVING BASICS

For some people, one of the scariest memories of childhood involves climbing the ladder to the high diving board at the local pool. So it's no wonder that in a 1939 national survey, Beatrice "Bee" Kyle was voted the most popular outdoor performer, male or female, in the United States.

Kyle was a high diver—a *really* high diver. Her claim to fame was plummeting more than 100 feet (30.5 m) toward an eight-foot-deep (2.4 m) tank of water. Though she was married to a lion tamer, it was Bee who was the biggest draw. People thought it took more courage to plummet through the sky than to stand next to a growling, sharp-toothed lion!

DIVING EVENTS

At competitions, the divers begin by jumping off a **platform** or a **springboard**. The platform is a flat, stable surface. Since platforms do not move, the diver simply hops off them. Springboards are typically lower than platforms. However, springboards allow the divers to launch themselves high into the air before falling to the water. At the Olympic Games, only the 10-meter (32 foot, 10 inch) platform and three-meter (9 foot, 10 inch) springboard are used. Other elite competitions also have a one-meter springboard competition.

Synchronized diving became an Olympic sport at the 2000 Games. In this event, two divers complete the same dive at the same time. The goal is for the divers to be synchronized, or the same. It can be done off a platform or a springboard.

DIVE CATEGORIES

There are several categories of dives. One is the **forward dive**, in which the diver faces and dives toward the pool. On the springboard, the diver starts at the back of

▲ *This springboard diver approaches the water for a backward dive.*

the board and moves toward the end before jumping. On the platform, the diver sometimes begins the dive while standing at the front end of the **tower.**

For a **backward dive**, the diver begins by facing the back of the board. She leads with the back of her head and shoulder blades as she launches herself toward the water. In a **reverse dive**, the diver faces the pool but rotates in the air backward toward the board. For an **inward dive**, the diver begins by facing the back of the board but rotates toward the board in midair to finish the dive. A diver can add twists to all of these categories.

Lastly, a platform diver can begin the dive by doing an armstand. This is also called a handstand. The diver's legs and feet must be completely motionless for three seconds before she pushes off the platform and completes her dive.

DIVE POSITIONS

There are also several key positions a diver might attempt to achieve before entering the water. For instance, a diver can attempt to hold her body in a straight position. She might also bend her body at the hips while keeping her legs straight. This maneuver is called the pike position. If a diver pulls her bent knees to her chest, she's getting in the tuck position. If a diver does a combination of these three maneuvers, she's performing a **free** dive, or a dive in the open position.

SCORING A DIVE

The winner of a diving competition is the one who has the highest score after a series of dives. In the Olympic Games, women dive five times in the championship round. There is also a preliminary and a semifinal round.

Determining the score of each dive can be complex, though. Every possible dive is assigned a degree of difficulty. The judges watch the dive and give it a score between zero and 10. At this stage the judges only consider the technique and grace of the dive. This includes the **takeoff**, the **flight**, and the **entry** into the water. There are seven judges in Olympic competition. The group's two highest and two lowest scores are removed and the remaining three scores are added together and then multiplied by the degree of difficulty. Dives are scored in half-point increments from zero to 10, with a perfect dive

Professional Competitions

Before each meet, a diver comes up with her own statement of dives, which is also called a dive list. It is exactly what it sounds like: a list of the dives she will perform at the meet. Do you think you could look at one of these lists and visualize what it means? What does a front one-and-a-half somersault with a twist look like? How about a reverse one-and-a-half somersault with a one-and-a-half twist?

▲ *Synchronized divers begin a dive off springboards.*

receiving a 10. This scoring system is used for all levels of competitive diving.

Synchronized diving uses 11 judges. Three of them judge the execution of Diver One, three judge the execution of Diver Two, and five judge the synchronization. The high and low scores for each of the execution marks are removed. The high and low marks from the synchronization scores are removed as well. The five remaining scores are added together and then divided by five. That

▲ *A diving aparatus with platforms and springboards*

number is then multiplied by three. Finally, that number is multiplied by the degree of difficulty.

DIVING EQUIPMENT

Technically, diving is a noncontact sport. If done improperly, though, it can easily feel like one when hitting the water. In fact, if a diver takes off from a 10-meter platform, she can be traveling at approximately 30 miles per hour (40 km/h) when she hits the water. The impact of a body hitting the water at that speed is strong enough to cause serious injury. That means it is very important to take proper precautions when practicing diving.

One way many divers do this is by using an overhead-mounted safety belt system. These devices are designed to harness a diver as she practices flipping and twisting in the air. Often the diver will use this system while jumping on a trampoline. It can also be designed to go over water. These safety rigs greatly reduce the risk of injury. They also allow the diver to work on parts of a dive over and over again.

Another piece of safety equipment is a sparging system, also known as a bubbler. These are located at the bottom of the pool. By forcing bursts of air into the pool, these devices create air bubbles that cushion a diver's contact with the water. Doing a back or belly flop into water cushioned with bubbles will still hurt, but not as much.

Evolving Equipment

Scoring a dive wasn't always as complicated as it is today. In 1904, when diving first became an Olympic sport, U.S. diver George Sheldon won the gold medal on the platform largely due to his smooth entries into the water. Germany protested his medal, unsuccessfully, claiming that his dives weren't difficult enough to earn gold. Ever since, the Olympic Games have used a mathematical scoring system that tries to weigh both degree of difficulty and degree of execution. Sometimes, perhaps, complicated *is* better. Check out FINA's website, www.fina.org, if you want to learn more about how to score a dive.

By using good equipment—and even more importantly, good judgment—a diver will be both safer and better prepared for her next competition.

THE APPEAL OF DIVING

Not only can diving be dangerous—it can be scary. However, with the proper preparations, diving is also an exciting and fun sport.

Laura Wilkinson won an Olympic gold medal on the 10-meter platform at the 2000 Olympic Games. She often smiles right before particularly difficult dives. Why? "I smile because I love what I do," she said. "I make a com-

▲ *Diving requires a unique combination of gracefulness, gymnastics, and courage.*

mitment before the competition to enjoy the experience however it turns out."

In fact, conquering one's fear is part of what makes diving fun. Several top divers suffered at some point from a fear of heights. By overcoming their fears, they went on to become some of the best divers in Olympic history.

▲ *Aileen Riggin became the youngest U.S. Olympic gold medalist when she won the springboard competition at the 1920 Games.*

CHAPTER 5
DIVING IN

Because swimming and diving both take place in the water, they've become linked together. But the history of competitive diving, also called fancy diving, starts with another sport: gymnastics.

During the 17th century, Sweden and Germany had successful gymnastics programs. During the summer, those gymnasts would move their equipment to the beach and perform their stunts and acrobatics over the water.

The history of high diving since then has not been documented as closely. However, there are written reports as far back as 1871 of people holding a diving competition off the London Bridge in England.

MODERN OLYMPIC GAMES

As with women's swimming, women's diving did not become an Olympic sport until 1912. The only women's diving event at those Olympic Games was the 10-meter platform. Sweden and Germany continued to have the strongest diving programs at the time. Two Swedes, Greta Johansson and Lisa Regnell, earned the gold and silver medals respectively at the 1912 Games.

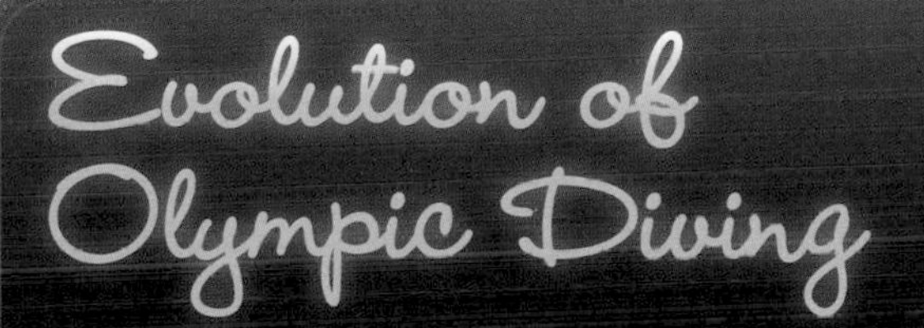

The 1912 Olympic Games were the first in which women could enter the 10-meter platform diving competition. In 1920, springboard diving was added to the women's program. These were the only two options for men and women until 2000, when synchronized diving—on both platform and springboard—was also added to the Olympic program.

There were no Olympic Games in 1916 due to World War I. When the Games resumed in 1920, the rest of the world had caught up to Sweden and Germany. The United States was emerging as a diving power, especially in the new three-meter springboard event. In fact, U.S. divers Aileen Riggin, Helen Wainwright, and Thelma Payne won all three medals in that event. In doing so, they helped set off an era of American diving dominance that lasted for more than eight decades.

By 2004, the United States had won almost half of the total medals handed out over the history of Olympic diving.

PAT MCCORMICK

Perhaps the most influential women's diver in history was an American named Pat McCormick. She was known for her absolute fearlessness when trying seemingly impossible dives.

Of course, McCormick wasn't actually fearless. She was more than willing to admit that she suffered from a fear of heights. McCormick certainly was courageous, though. As a teenager, she allowed strongmen to fling her as high as they could into the air. Strongmen were men who made money showing off their strength.

McCormick was also tough. At a medical examination in 1951, her doctor discovered that she had sustained

▲ *Pat McCormick demonstrates the dive that lead her to victory in the 1952 Olympic Games.*

many serious injuries during her career. They included a scalp wound half a foot long, scars at the base of her spine, and previously broken fingers and ribs. During at least one dive, she had hit her head on the diving board.

Yet none of these injuries prevented McCormick from continuing to attempt dives that no one else could do. In 1952 she won Olympic gold medals in both the springboard and platform competitions. In 1956, she repeated the feat. At the time, she became the first diver, male or female, to win both diving gold medals in consecutive Olympic Games.

Two of the dives McCormick was known for were her back dive and her forward one-and-a-half somersault with a twist. Both dives were considered technically difficult and hugely daring at the time.

Fu Mingxia prepares for the women's 3-meter springboard finals at the 1996 Olympic Games.

DOUBLE GOLDS

At the 1984 and 1988 Games, U.S. diver Greg Louganis became the second diver to win two diving gold medals in two consecutive Olympic Games. Nearly a decade later, Fu Mingxia of China almost pulled off the feat as well. At the 1992 Games, she took the gold on the 10-meter platform. At the 1996 Games, she won the gold medal on both the platform and three-meter springboard. At the 2000 Games, Fu won yet another gold on the springboard.

JENNIFER CHANDLER

When U.S. diver Jennifer Chandler began competing internationally, it seemed as if all people could talk about was her age. After all, she was only 14. "If one more person says 'And she's only 14'," Chandler announced at the time, "I think I'll scream."

By the time she was 17, the fans at the 1976 Olympic Games were screaming for Chandler as she won the gold medal on the three-meter springboard.

In 1977, while diving at Ohio State University, Chandler severely injured her back as she attempted a back two-and-a-half somersault tuck from the 10-meter platform. Two years later, in 1979, she reinjured her back. Chandler recovered just in time to qualify for the 1980 Olympic Games in Moscow. However, the United States boycotted the 1980 Games, and Chandler never got to dive in another Olympic Games.

▲ *Chinese diver, Gao Min executes her 1992 Olympic gold-medal-winning dive in the women's springboard finals.*

CHAPTER 6

PERFECT ENTRY

The U.S. diving team has historically been the best in the world. However, that began to change when China entered the Olympic diving competition for the first time in 1984. Ever since, China has dominated the sport at the Olympic level.

Chinese Dynasty

One of the ways China was able to develop into the elite women's diving country was by studying U.S. diver Greg Louganis, the man most consider to be the greatest diver of all time. China's national coaches pored over film of Louganis diving, then instructed their divers to mimic his movements and his technical skills. Louganis won all four events he competed in at the 1984 and 1988 Games, and the Chinese have won most of the medals since.

GAO MIN

Gao Min began diving at the age of nine. She didn't lose much after that. By age 13, Gao was the world champion in her age group on both the one-meter and three-meter springboards. In 1988, when she was 18 years old, she won the Olympic gold medal on the three-meter springboard.

China national team coach Xu Yiming credited Gao's success to hard work. "She is the first one in the pool and the last to leave," he said about practice.

Gao remained undefeated in world competitions on the three-meter springboard from 1986 to 1992. She was named Women's World Springboard Diver of the Year seven consecutive years.

Still, Gao considered retirement before the 1992 Olympic Games. But her coach encouraged her to give it one more go, so she did. A few months later she once again found herself standing on the podium with a gold medal.

FU MINGXIA

Gao was one of the first Chinese diving stars. She was hardly the only one, though. Between 1984 and 2008, Chinese divers won 11 of the 14 possible gold medals in individual diving events.

Perhaps the greatest Chinese diver was Fu Mingxia. The soft-spoken diver won the 10-meter platform event at the 1992 Olympic Games. She followed that with gold medals in both the platform and the springboard events at the 1996 Olympic Games. After a two-year retirement, Fu returned to the 2000 Olympic Games to earn a fourth gold medal while winning the three-meter springboard. She also won a silver medal in the three-meter synchronized springboard event with partner Guo Jingjing.

MARY ELLEN CLARK

The Chinese divers have been so good since 1984 that they haven't left many spots on the podium for anyone else. One U.S. diver who did have Olympic success was Mary Ellen Clark. In 1992, Clark grabbed the bronze medal on the 10-meter platform.

Three years later, though, her chances of winning another medal didn't look good. For some reason, she had

▲ *American diver Mary Ellen Clark competes in the 1996 U.S. Olympic diving trials.*

begun to experience intense bouts of vertigo. That condition made her dizzy whenever she stood on the platform. It got so bad that she finally had to spend nine months away from the pool. In that time she went through therapy to try to overcome the vertigo.

Clark was considered an extreme long shot going into the 1996 Olympic Games. However, she did have one thing going for her: The 1996 Games were on her home soil in Atlanta, Georgia.

With support from the home crowd and with the help of her coach, Ron O'Brien, Clark managed to claim another bronze medal on the 10-meter platform. To do it, she had to come from way behind twice during the competition.

Number One Fan

Mary Ellen Clark's father, Gene, needed to have major heart surgery in 1992 and did not get to watch her win her first bronze medal. Before the 1996 Olympic Games, Gene was diagnosed with cancer, but he was in the stands to see his daughter win her second bronze medal. "I'm glad he was here to see it because he deserves it," Clark said. "He was my first coach, and he's really my hero."

LAURA WILKINSON

Just three months before the 2000 Olympic Games in Sydney, Australia, U.S. diver Laura Wilkinson whacked her foot against some training equipment and broke three bones. She could have had surgery, but that would have sidelined her for weeks. Instead, she decided to wear a series of casts.

For a while, she couldn't safely dive into the water. So Wilkinson would climb to the top of the platform and stare down at the water. While up there, she would visualize the various stages of her dives. She would see her body tucking and untucking, going through all the proper motions. To the surprise of many, Wilkinson not only made it through the U.S. Olympic trials, but she *won* the trials.

For her third of five dives at the 2000 Games, Wilkinson did the same dive that had won the Olympic trials: a reverse two-and-a-half somersault with a tuck. She got

▲ *U.S. diver Laura Wilkinson competes at a 2004 diving competition in Athens, Greece.*

the same result. Her body barely made a splash as she entered the water. Each judge gave her a nine or better. The maximum score is 10.

That dive gave Wilkinson the lead in the 2000 Olympic Games, but there were still two dives to go. Her next dive was particularly difficult. It was an inward two-and-a-half somersault in the pike position. Earlier, in the preliminary round, Wilkinson had botched the dive. Now she had to find a way to correct her earlier mistakes.

That is exactly what she did. She emerged from the water with a smile and with excellent scores from the judges. "I knew I had it in me somewhere," she said later, referring to her dive. One round later, she had more than a dive to show for herself. She also had a gold medal. It was the first one a U.S. woman had received since 1976.

▲ *Natalie Coughlin smiles after setting a new U.S. record in the women's 200-meter backstroke at the 2002 U.S. championships.*

CHAPTER 7

PLAYING TO WIN

The competition in women's swimming and diving gets fiercer and fiercer every year. Part of this can be attributed to science. As we learn more about the human body, we gain a better understanding of its limits and how to push through them. Another part of it is participation. More and more athletes across the world are training with and against each other. Meanwhile, coaches are learning more. Equipment and facilities are improving as well. However, nobody achieves great success without the will to work hard, improve, and win.

NATALIE COUGHLIN

At 5-foot-8 (1.7 m), U.S. swimmer Natalie Coughlin is rarely the biggest or most imposing swimmer in the pool. But don't tell her that. As her former teammate Haley Cope said, "The thing about Natalie that cracks me up is in Natalie's head, she's like 6-foot-5 (2 m). She's always going, 'I'm as big as her,' and this girl is like eight inches (0.2 m) taller than Natalie and outweighs her by 50 pounds (22.7 kg). In Natalie's head, she's huge. And she swims that way."

In 2000, Coughlin tore a shoulder muscle and was unable to perform well at the 2000 Olympic trials. She seriously considered quitting. Instead, she accepted a **scholarship** to swim at the University of California and became arguably the most successful collegiate swimmer of all time.

When she arrived at the 2003 World Championships, she was expected to win several events. However, she suffered through a severe virus and didn't win a single individual race. Then the 2004 Olympic Games happened. Competing in Athens, Greece, Coughlin became one of only a handful of Americans in any sport to win five

Jenny Thompson swims the 100-meter freestyle in the 1992 Olympic Games in Barcelona.

JENNY THOMPSON

At the 2004 Olympic Games, U.S. swimmer Jenny Thompson won two silver medals. This was amazing for several reasons. For one thing, it meant that Thompson got to go home with multiple medals in four straight Olympic Games. More importantly, it brought her career medal count to 12, the most medals of any female swimmer in Olympic history. The final tally of her phenomenal career is eight golds, three silvers, and one bronze medal.

Olympic medals in a single Olympic Games. She won two gold medals, two silver medals, and one bronze. Finally, she had lived up to everyone's high expectations of her.

Everyone's, that is, except her own. Not satisfied, she trained for another four years. At the 2008 Games in Beijing, China, she won six more medals. That was the most medals won by any U.S. female in a single Olympic Games.

AMANDA BEARD

It did not take long for Amanda Beard to make an impact in the pool. The U.S. swimmer won three medals at the 1996 Olympic Games when she was 14 years old. She won a gold medal in the 4x100 medley relay as well as silver medals in the 100- and 200-meter breaststroke. Four years later, in 2000, Beard

▲ *Amanda Beard dives into the water for the women's 200-meter breaststroke at the 2008 Olympic Games.*

won a bronze medal in the 200-meter breaststroke. At the 2004 Olympic Games, Beard won a gold medal in the 200-meter breaststroke and two more silver medals. One was in the 200 IM, and the other was in the 4x100 medley relay.

Fame came along with success. Beard's outgoing personality made her as popular with the media as she was with her growing number of fans. Pictures of her graced all kinds of products and magazines. About the only one who didn't like Amanda Beard was . . . Amanda Beard.

Though she hid it from the world, Beard was suffering from bouts of depression. The pool was helping and hurting her at the same time.

Melissa Stockwell

In 2004, U.S. Army Lieutenant Melissa Stockwell was serving in Iraq when a roadside bomb hit her vehicle. Stockwell survived, but her left leg had to be amputated above the knee. She turned the life-altering injury into an opportunity, however, by using her rehab swimming work as her new battlefield. As an athlete and natural competitor, Stockwell worked diligently not only to recover, but to qualify for the 2008 Paralympic Games in Beijing, China. The Paralympic Games are an Olympic-style event for athletes with physical disabilities. There, she competed in three swimming events. Although she did not win any medals, her journey had been a success. "In my mind, I have made it to Beijing," she said, "and it was my goal in the first place."

At the 2008 Olympic Games, Beard didn't grab a single medal. It was the low point of her career. However, it was also the start of a new, better life.

For one, she gave birth to a son, Blaise. That changed her perspective on swimming. "It's just kind of amazing how he experiences pure joy in things that are so simple," she said. "It makes everything I used to think was a big deal not a big deal anymore."

Since then, Beard returned to the pool and is training again. Now, when she's not in the pool, she does her best to not think about it. When she *is* in the pool, though, her mind is very much on winning more Olympic medals.

▲ *Guo Jingjing (left) and Fu Mingxia pose with their gold medals in synchronized diving from the 2008 Olympic Games.*

GUO JINGJING

Guo Jingjing's diving career had a similar path as Gao Min's in the 1980s. Like Gao, Guo won almost every Olympic competition she entered. In fact, in the face of the 2012 Games, she had more medals than any female diver in Olympic history. Also like Gao, she considered retirement but finally decided against it.

"In 2004 I already won all the gold medals I could," she explained, "but I continued because in 2008 we were going to have the Games in our motherland."

Guo Jingjing's diving career might resemble Gao Min's, but that's where the similarities end. Unlike Gao, Guo is not only a diving star but also a celebrity. In her home country, China, she's as famous as the top football and baseball players are in the United States. Her name, face, and personal life appear everywhere in magazines and newspapers. She even is a spokesperson for McDonald's.

The 2008 Olympic Games were in Beijing, China. In front of her home crowd, Guo earned gold medals on the three-meter springboard and the synchronized three-meter springboard. In doing so, she tied Pat McCormick and Fu Mingxia for the most gold medals in Olympic women's diving history with four.

MARY BETH DUNNICHAY

Mary Beth Dunnichay first made the U.S. national team in 2006, as a 13-year-old. At the 2008 Olympic Games, the Indiana native was the youngest U.S. athlete in any sport to compete, at age 15. Her synchronized diving partner, Haley Ishimatsu, was the next youngest. The duo finished fifth in Beijing and continued to improve afterward.

In early 2011, Dunnichay teamed with Katherine Bell to win the national synchronized diving championship on the 10-meter platform. It was the third win in Dunnichay's young career.

Perhaps the most impressive evidence of her skill and talent, though, wasn't at the Olympic Games or nationals. It was at her high school state championship. After being homeschooled for several years, Dunnichay decided to attend a traditional high school. The experience was a positive one.

"Everyone treated me the same as anyone else," she said. "It was really cool."

After years of training six days a week, she also got to do things such as hang out with friends, go to movies, and join the cheerleading squad. She also joined the high school swimming and diving team. To fans and competitors, she was every bit an Olympian going back to high school.

Despite a sore shoulder that needed to be taped throughout the state tournament in 2011, Dunnichay shattered the state record for points scored. With a score of 544.05, she beat the second place finisher by 106 points. She also set a new Indiana state record by 40 points.

Over the long histories of competitive swimming and diving, there have been lots of great female athletes, and each one of them has had her own story to tell and her

Kelci Bryant

When Mary Beth Dunnichay broke the Indiana state high school diving record in 2011, she was breaking a record set by another top young U.S. diver. Kelci Bryant, along with partner Ariel Rittenhouse, placed fourth in the three-meter synchronized event at the 2008 Olympic Games in Beijing.

own obstacles to overcome. Some needed to prove to others that they deserved a chance to compete; others needed to convince themselves that they could be the best. Some showed us that they weren't too old to excel; others, that they weren't too young.

Maybe that's the coolest part about both swimming and diving. Old or young, big or small, if you have the willpower to keep diving into the pool, you might also have the willpower to conquer something you fear—or to achieve what right now seems impossible.

▲ *Mary Beth Dunnichay (right) and Haley Ishimatsu perform during the women's 10-meter synchronized event at the 2008 Olympic Games.*

GLOSSARY

backstroke: A swim stroke in which a swimmer lies on her back in the water. She scissor-kicks with her feet and alternates backward windmill-like arm pulls.

backward dive: The diver begins by facing the back of the board and rotates away from the board as she launches herself toward the water.

breaststroke: A swim stroke in which the swimmer mimics a frog's kick with her legs and feet.

butterfly: A swim stroke in which the swimmer uses her legs to mimic a dolphin's movement while her arms pull over the water, each in unison with the other.

doping: The use of illegal PEDs to help one's performance.

drag: The friction between swimmer and water. The more drag, the slower the swimmer's time.

entry: How the diver enters the water.

flight: How the diver executes her dive in the air.

flip turn: When swimmers in the front crawl and backstroke do a somersault and push off the wall with their feet.

forward dive: The diver faces and rotates toward the pool. On the springboard, the diver starts at the back of the board and moves toward the end of it.

free: Any combination of the dive positions.

front crawl: A swim stroke, also known as the freestyle, in which a swimmer scissor-kicks with her feet. She alternates her arms in a windmill-like motion.

individual medleys (IMs): When a swimmer performs more than one stroke in a race.

inward dive: The diver begins by facing the board but rotates toward the board, midair, to finish facing the pool.

lap: A swimmer swims to one end of the pool and back.

length: A swimmer swims from one end of the pool to the other.

medley: A race that includes all four swim strokes.

platform: One of two standard boards for diving. It does not move.

recover: When the hand exits the water at the end of the stroke and returns to the water in front of the swimmer.

reverse dive: The diver faces the pool but rotates, once in the air, toward the board.

scholarship: Money given to students to help them pay for classes or other college expenses as a reward for skills in specific areas, such as athletics.

springboard: One of two standard boards for diving. It propels divers into the air upon takeoff.

synchronized: The same movements at the same time.

takeoff: How the diver launches herself into the air.

tower: Another term for the diving platform apparatus.

FOR MORE INFORMATION

BOOKS

Crossingham, John. *Swimming in Action*. New York: Crabtree Pub. Co., 2003.
This book covers the basic swim strokes and includes a few games for the pool.

Evans, Janet. *Janet Evans' Total Swimming*. Champaign, IL: Human Kinetics, 2007.
Written by one of the greatest swimmers of all time, this book is meant for anyone who wants to swim competitively or just for fitness.

O'Brien, Ron. *Springboard and Platform Diving*. Champaign, IL: Human Kinetics, 2003.
Written by a legendary coach, this book tells you everything there is to know about competitive diving.

WEBSITES

FINA

www.fina.org

This is the official website of the *Fédération Internationale de Natation* (FINA), an international group that oversees water sports all over the world.

USA Diving

www.usadiving.org

This is the official website for the governing body of U.S. diving. It includes an essay on the history of diving and information on how to become a member of the team.

USA Swimming

www.usaswimming.org

This is the official website for the governing body of U.S. swimming. It includes training tips, member resources, and upcoming events.

INDEX

backstroke, 6, 9
Beard, Amanda, 50–51
Bell, Katherine, 54–55
Bleibtrey, Ethelda, 15
boycotts, 22
breaststroke, 6–7, 9, 14, 50–51
Bryant, Kelci, 55
butterfly, 6–7, 9

car accident, 19, 20
Caulkins, Tracy, 20–22
Chandler, Jennifer, 41
Clark, Mary Ellen, 44–45, 46
Coughlin, Natalie, 49–50

dive categories, 27–29
dive positions, 29
dive scoring, 30–33
diving safety, 33–34
doping, 23
Dunnichay, Mary Beth, 54–56
Durack, Fanny, 15, 16–17

Evans, Janet, 24–25

Fédération Internationale de Natation (FINA), 23, 34
Fraser, Dawn, 18–19, 20
freestyle, 5–6, 7, 9, 10, 12, 14, 16, 18–19, 25
front crawl, 5–6
Fu Mingxia, 40, 44, 54

Gao Min, 43–44, 53, 54
Guo Jingjing, 44, 53–54
gymnastics, 36–37

individual medley (IM), 10, 20, 21, 22, 25, 51
injury, 19, 33, 40–41, 52
International Swimming Hall of Fame, 16, 17
Ishimatsu, Haley, 54

Johansson, Greta, 37

Kyle, Beatrice "Bee", 26–27

Louganis, Greg, 40, 43

McCormick, Pat, 38–40, 54
medley, 7, 10, 20

Olympic Games, 8, 10, 15–16, 27, 30, 34, 38
  1904, 34
  1912, 16, 18, 37
  1920, 38
  1952, 40
  1956, 18, 22, 40
  1960, 18
  1964, 18, 19
  1968, 20
  1976, 22, 41
  1980, 20, 22, 41
  1984, 5, 21–22, 40, 42, 43

1988, 22–23, 25, 40, 43
1992, 25, 40, 43, 44
1996, 40, 44, 45, 50
2000, 27, 34, 37, 40, 44, 46–47, 50
2004, 49, 50, 51, 53
2008, 5, 50, 52, 53, 54, 55, 56
2012, 53
Olympic trials, 46–47
2000, 49
Otto, Kristin, 22–24

Payne, Thelma, 38
performance-enhancing drugs (PEDs), 23–24
platform, 27, 29, 33, 34, 37, 40, 44–45, 46, 55

Regnell, Lisa, 37
relays, 10, 22, 50–51
Riggin, Eileen, 38
Rittenhouse, Ariel, 56

springboard, 27–29, 37, 38, 40, 41, 43–44, 54
steroids, 23–24
Stockbauer, Hannah, 24
Stockwell, Melissa, 52
swimming events, 10
swimming races, 8–9
swimming strokes, 5–7
synchronized diving, 27, 31–33, 37, 54–55

Thompson, Jenny, 50
Torres, Dara, 4–5, 12

University of California, 49

van Almsick, Franziska, 24

Wainwright, Helen, 38
Wilkinson, Laura, 34–35, 46–47
World Championship
1978, 20
2003, 49
2007, 12
2009, 12

PLACES TO VISIT

International Swimming Hall of Fame

1 Hall of Fame Drive
Fort Lauderdale, FL 33316
(954) 462-6536
www.ishof.org
The International Swimming Hall of Fame enshrines the greatest moments and athletes in the history of water sports. Its website features video archives and a photo gallery.

US Olympic Training Center

One Olympic Plaza
Colorado Springs, CO 80909
(888) 659-8687 or (719) 866-4618
www.teamusa.org
The Olympic Training Center offers free public tours that include a video and a walking tour of the complex, showcasing the training facilities for the US Olympic and Paralympic hopefuls who train there.

ABOUT THE AUTHOR

Paul Hoblin is the author of several sports books for young adults. He lives in St. Paul, Minnesota. A few summers ago he finally figured out how to do a flip turn.

ABOUT THE CONTENT CONSULTANT

At the 1976 Olympic Games, John Naber earned one silver and four gold medals in swimming. He has covered swimming and diving as a television announcer, and produced and starred in a swimming instructional video. He lives in Pasadena, California.